Other Books by Richard Bach

Jonathan Livingston Seagull
a story

RICHARD BACH

PHOTOGRAPHS BY RUSSELL MUNSON

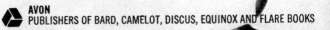

AVON
PUBLISHERS OF BARD, CAMELOT, DISCUS, EQUINOX AND FLARE BOOKS

To the real Jonathan Seagull,
who lives within us all

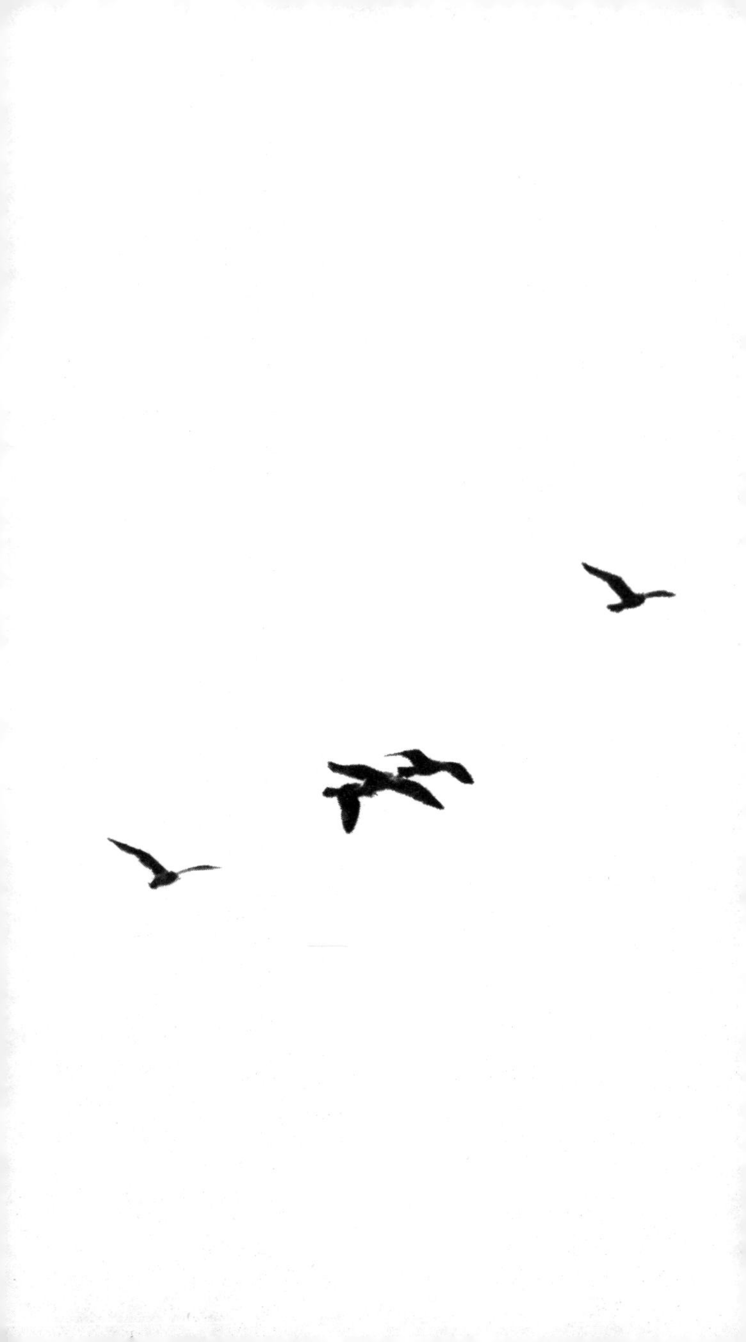

Part One

It was morning, and the new sun sparkled gold across the ripples of a gentle sea.

A mile from shore a fishing boat chummed the water, and the word for Breakfast Flock flashed through the air, till a crowd of a thousand seagulls came to dodge and fight for bits of food. It was another busy day beginning.

But way off alone, out by himself beyond boat and shore, Jonathan Livingston Seagull was practicing. A hundred feet in the sky he lowered his webbed feet, lifted his beak, and strained to hold a painful hard twisting curve through his wings. The curve meant that he would fly slowly, and now he slowed until the wind was a whisper in his face, until the ocean stood still beneath him. He narrowed his eyes in fierce concentration, held his breath, forced one . . . single . . . more . . . inch . . . of . . . curve. . . . Then his feathers ruffled, he stalled and fell.

Seagulls, as you know, never falter, never stall. To stall in the air is for them disgrace and it is dishonor.

But Jonathan Livingston Seagull, unashamed, stretching his wings again in that trembling hard curve—slowing, slowing, and stalling once more—was no ordinary bird.

Most gulls don't bother to learn more than the simplest facts of flight—how to get from shore to food and back again. For most gulls, it is not flying that matters, but eating. For this gull, though, it was not eating that mattered, but flight. More than anything else, Jonathan Livingston Seagull loved to fly.

This kind of thinking, he found, is not the way to make one's self popular with other birds. Even his parents were dismayed as Jonathan spent whole days alone, making hundreds of low-level glides, experimenting.

He didn't know why, for instance, but when he flew at altitudes less than half his wingspan above the water, he could stay in the air longer, with less effort. His glides ended not with the usual feet-down splash into the sea, but with a long flat wake as he touched the surface with his feet tightly streamlined against his body. When he began sliding in to feet-up landings on the beach, then pacing the length of his slide in the sand, his parents were very much dismayed indeed.

"Why, Jon, *why?*" his mother asked. "Why is it so hard to be like the rest of the flock, Jon? Why can't you leave low flying to the pelicans, the albatross? Why don't you *eat?* Son, you're bone and feathers!"

"I don't mind being bone and feathers,

mom. I just want to know what I can do in the air and what I can't, that's all. I just want to know."

"See here, Jonathan," said his father, not unkindly. "Winter isn't far away. Boats will be few, and the surface fish will be swimming deep. If you must study, then study food, and how to get it. This flying business is all very well, but you can't eat a glide, you know. Don't you forget that the reason you fly is to eat."

Jonathan nodded obediently. For the next few days he tried to behave like the other gulls; he really tried, screeching and fighting with the flock around the piers and fishing boats, diving on scraps of fish and bread. But he couldn't make it work.

It's all so pointless, he thought, deliberately dropping a hard-won anchovy to a hungry old gull chasing him. I could be spending all this time learning to fly. There's so much to learn!

It wasn't long before Jonathan Gull was off by himself again, far out at sea, hungry, happy, learning.

The subject was speed, and in a week's practice he learned more about speed than the fastest gull alive.

From a thousand feet, flapping his wings as hard as he could, he pushed over into a blazing steep dive toward the waves, and learned why seagulls don't make blazing steep power-dives. In just six seconds he was moving seventy miles per hour, the speed at which one's wing goes unstable on the upstroke.

Time after time it happened. Careful as he was, working at the very peak of his ability, he lost control at high speed.

Climb to a thousand feet. Full power straight ahead first, then push over, flapping, to a vertical dive. Then, every time, his left wing stalled on an upstroke, he'd roll violently left, stall his right wing recovering, and flick like fire into a wild tumbling spin to the right.

He couldn't be careful enough on that upstroke. Ten times he tried, and all ten times, as he passed through seventy miles per hour, he burst into a churning mass of feathers, out of control, crashing down into the water.

The key, he thought at last, dripping wet, must be to hold the wings still at high speeds—to flap up to fifty and then hold the wings still.

From two thousand feet he tried again, rolling into his dive, beak straight down, wings full out and stable from the moment he passed fifty miles per hour. It took tremendous strength, but it worked. In ten seconds he had blurred through ninety miles per hour. Jonathan had set a world speed record for seagulls!

But victory was short-lived. The instant he began his pullout, the instant he changed the angle of his wings, he snapped into that same terrible uncontrolled disaster, and at ninety miles per hour it hit him like dynamite. Jonathan Seagull exploded in midair and smashed down into a brick-hard sea.

When he came to, it was well after dark, and he floated in moonlight on the surface of the ocean. His wings were ragged bars of lead, but the weight of failure was even heavier on his back. He wished, feebly, that the weight could be just enough to drag him gently down to the bottom, and end it all.

As he sank low in the water, a strange hollow voice sounded within him. There's no way around it. I am a seagull. I am limited by my nature. If I were meant to learn so much about flying, I'd have charts for brains. If I were meant to fly at speed, I'd have a falcon's short wings, and live on mice instead of fish. My father was right. I must forget this foolishness. I must fly home to the Flock and be content as I am, as a poor limited seagull.

The voice faded, and Jonathan agreed. The place for a seagull at night is on shore, and from this moment forth, he vowed, he would be a normal gull. It would make everyone happier.

He pushed wearily away from the dark water and flew toward the land, grateful for what he had learned about work-saving low-altitude flying.

But no, he thought. I am done with the way I was, I am done with everything I learned. I am a seagull like every other seagull, and I will fly like one. So he climbed painfully to a hundred feet and flapped his wings harder, pressing for shore.

He felt better for his decision to be just

another one of the Flock. There would be no ties now to the force that had driven him to learn, there would be no more challenge and no more failure. And it was pretty, just to stop thinking, and fly through the dark, toward the lights above the beach.

Dark! The hollow voice cracked in alarm. *Seagulls never fly in the dark!*

Jonathan was not alert to listen. It's pretty, he thought. The moon and the lights twinkling on the water, throwing out little beacon-trails through the night, and all so peaceful and still. . . .

Get down! Seagulls never fly in the dark! If you were meant to fly in the dark, you'd have the eyes of an owl! You'd have charts for brains! You'd have a falcon's short wings!

There in the night, a hundred feet in the air, Jonathan Livingston Seagull—blinked. His pain, his resolutions, vanished.

Short wings. *A falcon's short wings!*

That's the answer! What a fool I've been! All I need is a tiny little wing, all I need is to fold most of my wings and fly on just the tips alone! *Short wings!*

He climbed two thousand feet above the black sea, and without a moment for thought of failure and death, he brought his forewings tightly in to his body, left only the narrow swept daggers of his wingtips extended into the wind, and fell into a vertical dive.

The wind was a monster roar at his head. Seventy miles per hour, ninety, a hundred and twenty and faster still. The wing-strain now at a hundred and forty miles per hour wasn't nearly as hard as it had been before at seventy, and with the faintest twist of his wingtips he eased out of the dive and shot above the waves, a gray cannonball under the moon.

He closed his eyes to slits against the wind

and rejoiced. A hundred forty miles per hour! And under control! If I dive from five thousand feet instead of two thousand, I wonder how fast . . .

His vows of a moment before were forgotten, swept away in that great swift wind. Yet he felt guiltless, breaking the promises he had made himself. Such promises are only for the gulls that accept the ordinary. One who has touched excellence in his learning has no need of that kind of promise.

By sunup, Jonathan Gull was practicing again. From five thousand feet the fishing boats were specks in the flat blue water, Breakfast Flock was a faint cloud of dust motes, circling.

He was alive, trembling ever so slightly with delight, proud that his fear was under control. Then without ceremony he hugged in his forewings, extended his short, angled wingtips, and plunged directly toward the sea. By the time he passed four thousand feet he had reached terminal velocity, the wind was a solid beating wall of sound against which he could move no faster. He was flying now straight down, at two hundred fourteen miles per hour. He swallowed, knowing that if his wings unfolded at that speed he'd be blown into a million tiny shreds of seagull. But the speed was power, and the speed was joy, and the speed was pure beauty.

He began his pullout at a thousand feet, wingtips thudding and blurring in that gigantic wind, the boat and the crowd of gulls tilting and growing meteor-fast, directly in his path.

He couldn't stop; he didn't know yet even how to turn at that speed.

Collision would be instant death.

And so he shut his eyes.

It happened that morning, then, just after sunrise, that Jonathan Livingston Seagull fired directly through the center of Breakfast Flock, ticking off two hundred twelve miles per hour, eyes closed, in a great roaring shriek of wind and feathers. The Gull of Fortune smiled upon him this once, and no one was killed.

By the time he had pulled his beak straight up into the sky he was still scorching along at a hundred and sixty miles per hour. When he had slowed to twenty and stretched his wings again at last, the boat was a crumb on the sea, four thousand feet below.

His thought was triumph. Terminal velocity! A seagull at *two hundred fourteen miles per hour!* It was a breakthrough, the greatest single moment in the history of the Flock, and in that moment a new age opened for Jonathan Gull. Flying out to his lonely practice area, folding his wings for a dive from eight thousand feet, he set himself at once to discover how to turn.

A single wingtip feather, he found, moved

a fraction of an inch, gives a smooth sweeping curve at tremendous speed. Before he learned this, however, he found that moving more than one feather at that speed will spin you like a rifle ball . . . and Jonathan had flown the first aerobatics of any seagull on earth.

He spared no time that day for talk with other gulls, but flew on past sunset. He discovered the loop, the slow roll, the point roll, the inverted spin, the gull bunt, the pinwheel.

When Jonathan Seagull joined the Flock on the beach, it was full night. He was dizzy and terribly tired. Yet in delight he flew a loop to landing, with a snap roll just before touchdown. When they hear of it, he thought, of the Breakthrough, they'll be wild with joy. How much more there is now to living! Instead of our drab slogging forth and back to the fishing boats, there's a reason to life! We can lift ourselves out of ignorance, we can find ourselves as creatures of excellence and intelligence and skill. We can be free! *We can learn to fly!*

The years ahead hummed and glowed with promise.

The gulls were flocked into the Council Gathering when he landed, and apparently had been so flocked for some time. They were, in fact, waiting.

"Jonathan Livingston Seagull! Stand to Center!" The Elder's words sounded in a voice of highest ceremony. Stand to Center meant only great shame or great honor. Stand to Center for Honor was the way the gulls' foremost leaders were marked. Of course, he thought, the Breakfast Flock this morning; they saw the Breakthrough! But I want no honors. I have no wish to be leader. I want only to share what I've found, to show those horizons out ahead for us all. He stepped forward.

"Jonathan Livingston Seagull," said the Elder, "Stand to Center for Shame in the sight of your fellow gulls!"

It felt like being hit with a board. His knees went weak, his feathers sagged, there was roaring in his ears. Centered for shame? Impossible! The Breakthrough! They can't understand! They're wrong, they're wrong!

". . . for his reckless irresponsibility," the solemn voice intoned, "violating the dignity and tradition of the Gull Family . . ."

To be centered for shame meant that he would be cast out of gull society, banished to a solitary life on the Far Cliffs.

". . . one day, Jonathan Livingston Seagull, you shall learn that irresponsibility does not pay. Life is the unknown and the unknowable, except that we are put into this world to eat, to stay alive as long as we possibly can."

A seagull never speaks back to the Council Flock, but it was Jonathan's voice raised. "Irresponsibility? My brothers!" he cried. "Who is more responsible than a gull who finds and follows a meaning, a higher purpose for life? For a thousand years we have scrabbled after fish heads, but now we have a reason to live—to learn, to discover, to be free! Give me one chance, let me show you what I've found . . ."

The Flock might as well have been stone.

"The Brotherhood is broken," the gulls intoned together, and with one accord they solemnly closed their ears and turned their backs upon him.

Jonathan Seagull spent the rest of his days alone, but he flew way out beyond the Far Cliffs. His one sorrow was not solitude, it was that other gulls refused to believe the glory of flight that awaited them; they refused to open their eyes and see.

He learned more each day. He learned that a streamlined high-speed dive could bring him to find the rare and tasty fish that schooled ten feet below the surface of the ocean: he no longer needed fishing boats and stale bread for survival. He learned to sleep in the air, setting a course at night across the offshore wind, covering a hundred miles from sunset to sunrise. With the same inner control, he flew through heavy sea-fogs and climbed above them into dazzling clear skies . . . in the very times when every other gull stood on the ground, knowing nothing but mist and rain. He learned to ride the high winds far inland, to dine there on delicate insects.

What he had once hoped for the Flock, he now gained for himself alone; he learned to fly, and was not sorry for the price that he had paid. Jonathan Seagull discovered that boredom and fear and anger are the reasons that a gull's life is so short, and with these gone from his thought, he lived a long fine life indeed.

They came in the evening, then, and found Jonathan gliding peaceful and alone through his beloved sky. The two gulls that appeared at his wings were pure as starlight, and the glow from them was gentle and friendly in the high night air. But most lovely of all was the skill with which they flew, their wingtips moving a precise and constant inch from his own.

Without a word, Jonathan put them to his test, a test that no gull had ever passed. He twisted his wings, slowed to a single mile per hour above stall. The two radiant birds slowed with him, smoothly, locked in position. They knew about slow flying.

He folded his wings, rolled and dropped in a dive to a hundred ninety miles per hour. They dropped with him, streaking down in flawless formation.

At last he turned that speed straight up into a long vertical slow-roll. They rolled with him, smiling.

He recovered to level flight and was quiet for a time before he spoke. "Very well," he said, "who are you?"

"We're from your Flock, Jonathan. We are your brothers." The words were strong and calm. "We've come to take you higher, to take you home."

"Home I have none. Flock I have none. I am Outcast. And we fly now at the peak of the Great Mountain Wind. Beyond a few hundred feet, I can lift this old body no higher."

"But you can, Jonathan. For you have learned. One school is finished, and the time has come for another to begin."

As it had shined across him all his life, so understanding lighted that moment for Jonathan Seagull. They were right. He *could* fly higher, and it *was* time to go home.

He gave one last look across the sky, across that magnificent silver land where he had learned so much.

"I'm ready," he said at last.

And Jonathan Livingston Seagull rose with the two star-bright gulls to disappear into a perfect dark sky.

Part Two

So this is heaven,
he thought, and he had to smile at himself. It was hardly respectful to analyze heaven in the very moment that one flies up to enter it.

As he came from Earth now, above the clouds and in close formation with the two brilliant gulls, he saw that his own body was growing as bright as theirs. True, the same young Jonathan Seagull was there that had always lived behind his golden eyes, but the outer form had changed.

It felt like a seagull body, but already it flew far better than his old one had ever flown. Why, with half the effort, he thought, I'll get twice the speed, twice the performance of my best days on Earth!

His feathers glowed brilliant white now,

and his wings were smooth and perfect as sheets of polished silver. He began, delightedly, to learn about them, to press power into these new wings.

At two hundred fifty miles per hour he felt that he was nearing his level-flight maximum speed. At two hundred seventy-three he thought that he was flying as fast as he could fly, and he was ever so faintly disappointed. There was a limit to how much the new body could do, and though it was much faster than his old level-flight record, it was still a limit that would take great effort to crack. In heaven, he thought, there should be no limits.

The clouds broke apart, his escorts called, "Happy landings, Jonathan," and vanished into thin air.

He was flying over a sea, toward a jagged shoreline. A very few seagulls were working the updrafts on the cliffs. Away off to the north, at the horizon itself, flew a few others. New sights, new thoughts, new questions. Why so few gulls? Heaven should be *flocked* with gulls! And why am I so tired, all at once? Gulls in heaven are never supposed to be tired, or to sleep.

Where had he heard that? The memory of his life on Earth was falling away. Earth had been a place where he had learned much, of course, but the details were blurred—something about fighting for food, and being Outcast.

The dozen gulls by the shoreline came to meet him, none saying a word. He felt only that he was welcome and that this was home. It had been a big day for him, a day whose sunrise he no longer remembered.

He turned to land on the beach, beating his wings to stop an inch in the air, then dropping lightly to the sand. The other gulls landed too, but not one of them so much as flapped a feather. They swung into the wind, bright wings outstretched, then somehow they changed the curve of their feathers until they had stopped in the same instant their feet touched the ground. It was beautiful control, but now Jonathan was just too tired to try it. Standing there on the beach, still without a word spoken, he was asleep.

In the days that followed, Jonathan saw that there was as much to learn about flight in this place as there had been in the life behind him. But with a difference. Here were gulls who thought as he thought. For each of them, the most important thing in living was to reach out and touch perfection in that which they most loved to do, and that was to fly. They were magnificent birds, all of them, and they spent hour after hour every day practicing flight, testing advanced aeronautics.

For a long time Jonathan forgot about the world that he had come from, that place where the Flock lived with its eyes tightly shut to the joy of flight, using its wings as means to the end of finding and fighting for food. But now and then, just for a moment, he remembered.

He remembered it one morning when he was out with his instructor, while they rested on the beach after a session of folded-wing snap rolls.

"Where is everybody, Sullivan?" he asked silently, quite at home now with the easy telepathy that these gulls used instead of screes and gracks. "Why aren't there more of us here? Why, where I came from there were . . ."

". . . thousands and thousands of gulls. I know." Sullivan shook his head. "The only answer I can see, Jonathan, is that you are pretty well a one-in-a-million bird. Most of us came along ever so slowly. We went from one world into another that was almost exactly like it, forgetting right away where we had come from, not caring where we were headed, living for the moment. Do you have any idea how many lives we must have gone through before we even got the first idea that there is more to life than eating, or fighting, or power in the Flock? A thousand lives, Jon, ten thousand! And then another hundred lives until we began to learn that there is such a thing as perfection, and another hundred again to get the idea that our purpose for living is to find that perfection and show it forth. The same rule holds for us now, of course: we choose our next world through what we learn in this one. Learn nothing, and the next world is the same as this one, all the same limitations and lead weights to overcome."

He stretched his wings and turned to face the wind. "But you, Jon," he said, "learned so much at one time that you didn't have to go through a thousand lives to reach this one."

In a moment they were airborne again, practicing. The formation point-rolls were difficult, for through the inverted half Jonathan had to think upside down, reversing the curve of his wing, and reversing it exactly in harmony with his instructor's.

"Let's try it again," Sullivan said, over and over: "Let's try it again." Then, finally, "Good." And they began practicing outside loops.

One evening the gulls that were not night-flying stood together on the sand, thinking. Jonathan took all his courage in hand and walked to the Elder Gull, who, it was said, was soon to be moving beyond this world.

"Chiang . . ." he said, a little nervously.

The old seagull looked at him kindly. "Yes, my son?" Instead of being enfeebled by age, the Elder had been empowered by it; he could outfly any gull in the Flock, and he had learned skills that the others were only gradually coming to know.

"Chiang, this world isn't heaven at all, is it?"

The Elder smiled in the moonlight. "You are learning again, Jonathan Seagull," he said.

"Well, what happens from here? Where are we going? Is there no such place as heaven?"

"No, Jonathan, there is no such place. Heaven is not a place, and it is not a time. Heaven is being perfect." He was silent for a moment. "You are a very fast flier, aren't you?"

"I . . . I enjoy speed," Jonathan said, taken aback but proud that the Elder had noticed.

"You will begin to touch heaven, Jonathan, in the moment that you touch perfect speed.

And that isn't flying a thousand miles an hour, or a million, or flying at the speed of light. Because any number is a limit, and perfection doesn't have limits. Perfect speed, my son, is being there."

Without warning, Chiang vanished and appeared at the water's edge fifty feet away, all in the flicker of an instant. Then he vanished again and stood, in the same millisecond, at Jonathan's shoulder. "It's kind of fun," he said.

Jonathan was dazzled. He forgot to ask about heaven. "How do you do that? What does it feel like? How far can you go?"

"You can go to any place and to any time that you wish to go," the Elder said. "I've gone everywhere and everywhen I can think of." He looked across the sea. "It's strange. The gulls who scorn perfection for the sake of travel go nowhere, slowly. Those who put aside travel for the sake of perfection go anywhere, instantly. Remember, Jonathan, heaven isn't a place or a time, because place and time are so very meaningless. Heaven is . . ."

"Can you teach me to fly like that?" Jonathan Seagull trembled to conquer another unknown.

"Of course, if you wish to learn."

"I wish. When can we start?"

"We could start now, if you'd like."

"I want to learn to fly like that," Jonathan

said, and a strange light glowed in his eyes. "Tell me what to do."

Chiang spoke slowly and watched the younger gull ever so carefully. "To fly as fast as thought, to anywhere that is," he said, "you must begin by knowing that you have already arrived . . ."

The trick, according to Chiang, was for Jonathan to stop seeing himself as trapped inside a limited body that had a forty-two-inch wingspan and performance that could be plotted on a chart. The trick was to know that his true nature lived, as perfect as an unwritten number, everywhere at once across space and time.

Jonathan kept at it, fiercely, day after day, from before sunrise till past midnight. And for all his effort he moved not a feather-width from his spot.

"Forget about faith!" Chiang said it time and again. "You didn't need faith to fly, you needed to understand flying. This is just the same. Now try again . . ."

Then one day Jonathan, standing on the shore, closing his eyes, concentrating, all in a flash knew what Chiang had been telling him. "Why, that's true! I *am* a perfect, unlimited gull!" He felt a great shock of joy.

"Good!" said Chiang, and there was victory in his voice.

Jonathan opened his eyes. He stood alone with the Elder on a totally different seashore—trees down to the water's edge, twin yellow suns turning overhead.

"At last you've got the idea," Chiang said, "but your control needs a little work . . ."

Jonathan was stunned. "Where are we?"

Utterly unimpressed with the strange surroundings, the Elder brushed the question aside. "We're on some planet, obviously, with a green sky and a double star for a sun."

Jonathan made a scree of delight, the first sound he had made since he had left Earth. "IT WORKS!"

"Well, of course it works, Jon," said Chiang. "It always works, when you know what you're doing. Now about your control . . ."

By the time they returned, it was dark. The other gulls looked at Jonathan with awe in their golden eyes, for they had seen him disappear from where he had been rooted for so long.

He stood their congratulations for less than a minute. "I'm the newcomer here! I'm just beginning! It is I who must learn from you!"

"I wonder about that, Jon," said Sullivan, standing near. "You have less fear of learning than any gull I've seen in ten thousand years." The Flock fell silent, and Jonathan fidgeted in embarrassment.

"We can start working with time if you wish," Chiang said, "till you can fly the past and the future. And then you will be ready to begin the most difficult, the most powerful, the most fun of all. You will be ready to begin to fly up and know the meaning of kindness and of love."

A month went by, or something that felt about like a month, and Jonathan learned at a tremendous rate. He always had learned quickly from ordinary experience, and now, the special student of the Elder Himself, he took in new ideas like a streamlined feathered computer.

But then the day came that Chiang vanished. He had been talking quietly with them all, exhorting them never to stop their learning and their practicing and their striving to understand more of the perfect invisible principle of all life. Then, as he spoke, his feathers went brighter and brighter and at last turned so brilliant that no gull could look upon him.

"Jonathan," he said, and these were the last words that he spoke, "keep working on love."

When they could see again, Chiang was gone.

As the days went past, Jonathan found himself thinking time and again of the Earth from which he had come. If he had known there just a tenth, just a hundredth, of what he knew here, how much more life would have meant! He stood on the sand and fell to wondering if there was a gull back there who might be struggling to break out of his limits, to see the meaning of flight beyond a way of travel to get a breadcrumb from a rowboat. Perhaps there might even have been one made Outcast for speaking his truth in the face of the Flock. And the more Jonathan practiced his kindness lessons, and the more he worked to know the nature of love, the more he wanted to go back to Earth. For in spite of his lonely past, Jonathan Seagull was born to be an instructor, and his own way of demonstrating love was to give something of the truth that he had seen to a gull who asked only a chance to see truth for himself.

Sullivan, adept now at thought-speed flight and helping the others to learn, was doubtful.

"Jon, you were Outcast once. Why do you think that any of the gulls in your old time would listen to you now? You know the proverb, and it's true: *The gull sees farthest who flies highest.* Those gulls where you came from are standing on the ground, squawking and fighting among themselves. They're a thousand miles from heaven—and you say you want to show them heaven from where they stand! Jon, they can't see their own wingtips! Stay here.

Help the new gulls here, the ones who are high enough to see what you have to tell them." He was quiet for a moment, and then he said, "What if Chiang had gone back to *his* old worlds? Where would you have been today?"

The last point was the telling one, and Sullivan was right. *The gull sees farthest who flies highest.*

Jonathan stayed and worked with the new birds coming in, who were all very bright and quick with their lessons. But the old feeling came back, and he couldn't help but think that there might be one or two gulls back on Earth who would be able to learn, too. How much more would he have known by now if Chiang had come to him on the day that he was Outcast!

"Sully, I must go back," he said at last. "Your students are doing well. They can help you bring the newcomers along."

Sullivan sighed, but he did not argue. "I think I'll miss you, Jonathan," was all he said.

"Sully, for shame!" Jonathan said in reproach, "and don't be foolish! What are we trying to practice every day? If our friendship depends on things like space and time, then when we finally overcome space and time, we've destroyed our own brotherhood! But overcome space, and all we have left is Here. Overcome time, and all we have left is Now. And in the middle of Here and Now, don't you think that we might see each other once or twice?"

Sullivan Seagull laughed in spite of himself. "You crazy bird," he said kindly. "If anybody can show someone on the ground how to see a thousand miles, it will be Jonathan Livingston Seagull." He looked at the sand. "Good-bye, Jon, my friend."

"Good-bye, Sully. We'll meet again." And

with that, Jonathan held in thought an image of the great gull-flocks on the shore of another time, and he knew with practiced ease that he was not bone and feather but a perfect idea of freedom and flight, limited by nothing at all.

Fletcher Lynd Seagull was still quite young, but already he knew that no bird had ever been so harshly treated by any Flock, or with so much injustice.

"I don't care what they say," he thought fiercely, and his vision blurred as he flew out toward the Far Cliffs. "There's so much more to flying than just flapping around from place to place! A . . . a . . . *mosquito* does that! One little barrel-roll around the Elder Gull, just for fun, and I'm Outcast! Are they blind? Can't they see? Can't they think of the glory that it'll be when we really learn to fly?

"I don't care what they think. I'll show

them what flying is! I'll be pure Outlaw, if that's the way they want it. And I'll make them so sorry . . ."

The voice came inside his own head, and though it was very gentle, it startled him so much that he faltered and stumbled in the air.

"Don't be harsh on them, Fletcher Seagull. In casting you out, the other gulls have only hurt themselves, and one day they will know this, and one day they will see what you see. Forgive them, and help them to understand."

An inch from his right wingtip flew the most brilliant white gull in all the world, gliding effortlessly along, not moving a feather, at what was very nearly Fletcher's top speed.

There was a moment of chaos in the young bird.

"What's going on? Am I mad? Am I dead? What is this?"

Low and calm, the voice went on within

his thought, demanding an answer. "Fletcher Lynd Seagull, do you want to fly?"

"YES, I WANT TO FLY!"

"Fletcher Lynd Seagull, do you want to fly so much that you will forgive the Flock, and learn, and go back to them one day and work to help them know?"

There was no lying to this magnificent skillful being, no matter how proud or how hurt a bird was Fletcher Seagull.

"I do," he said softly.

"Then, Fletch," that bright creature said to him, and the voice was very kind, "let's begin with Level Flight. . . ."

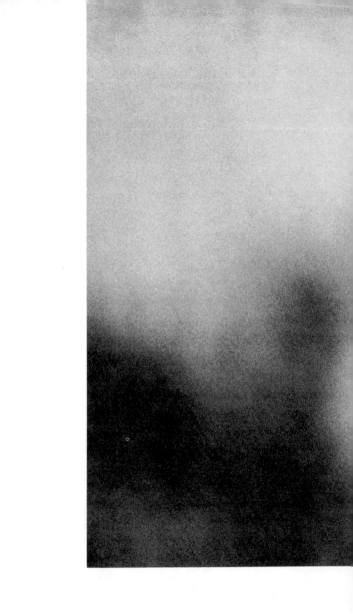

Part Three

Jonathan circled slowly
over the Far Cliffs, watching. This rough young
Fletcher Gull was very nearly a perfect flight-
student. He was strong and light and quick in
the air, but far and away more important, he
had a blazing drive to learn to fly.

Here he came this minute, a blurred gray
shape roaring out of a dive, flashing one hundred fifty miles per hour past his instructor. He
pulled abruptly into another try at a sixteen-
point vertical slow roll, calling the points out
loud.

". . . eight . . . nine . . . ten . . . see-
Jonathan-I'm-running-out-of-airspeed . . . elev-
en . . . I-want-good-sharp-stops-like-yours . . .
twelve . . . but-blast-it-I-just-can't-make . . .
thirteen . . . these-last-three-points . . . without . . . fourtee . . . *aaakk!*"

Fletcher's whipstall at the top was all the worse for his rage and fury at failing. He fell backward, tumbled, slammed savagely into an inverted spin, and recovered at last, panting, a hundred feet below his instructor's level.

"You're wasting your time with me, Jonathan! I'm too dumb! I'm too stupid! I try and try, but I'll never get it!"

Jonathan Seagull looked down at him and nodded. "You'll never get it for sure as long as you make that pullup so hard. Fletcher, you lost forty miles an hour in the entry! You *have* to be smooth! Firm but smooth, remember?"

He dropped down to the level of the younger gull. "Let's try it together now, in formation. And pay attention to that pullup. It's a smooth, easy entry."

By the end of three months Jonathan had six other students, Outcasts all, yet curious about this strange new idea of flight for the joy of flying.

Still, it was easier for them to practice high performance than it was to understand the reason behind it.

"Each of us is in truth an idea of the Great Gull, an unlimited idea of freedom," Jonathan would say in the evenings on the beach, "and precision flying is a step toward expressing our real nature. Everything that limits us we have to put aside. That's why all this high-speed practice, and low-speed, and aerobatics . . ."

. . . and his students would be asleep, exhausted from the day's flying. They liked the practice, because it was fast and exciting and it fed a hunger for learning that grew with every lesson. But not one of them, not even Fletcher Lynd Gull, had come to believe that the flight of ideas could possibly be as real as the flight of wind and feather.

"Your whole body, from wingtip to wing-tip," Jonathan would say, other times, "is nothing more than your thought itself, in a form you can see. Break the chains of your thought, and you break the chains of your body, too. . . ." But no matter how he said it, it sounded like pleasant fiction, and they needed more to sleep.

It was only a month later that Jonathan said the time had come to return to the Flock.

"We're not ready!" said Henry Calvin Gull. "We're not welcome! We're Outcast! We can't force ourselves to go where we're not welcome, can we?"

"We're free to go where we wish and to be what we are," Jonathan answered, and he lifted from the sand and turned east, toward the home grounds of the Flock.

There was brief anguish among his students, for it is the Law of the Flock that an Outcast never returns, and the Law had not been broken once in ten thousand years. The Law said stay; Jonathan said go; and by now he was a mile across the water. If they waited much longer, he would reach a hostile Flock alone.

"Well, we don't have to obey the law if we're not a part of the Flock, do we?" Fletcher said, rather self-consciously. "Besides, if there's a fight, we'll be a lot more help there than here."

And so they flew in from the west that morning, eight of them in a double-diamond formation, wingtips almost overlapping. They came across the Flock's Council Beach at a hundred thirty-five miles per hour, Jonathan in the lead, Fletcher smoothly at his right wing, Henry Calvin struggling gamely at his left. Then the whole formation rolled slowly to the right, as one bird . . . level . . . to . . . inverted . . . to . . . level, the wind whipping over them all.

The squawks and grockles of everyday life in the Flock were cut off as though the formation were a giant knife, and eight thousand gull-eyes watched, without a single blink. One by one, each of the eight birds pulled sharply upward into a full loop and flew all the way around to a dead-slow stand-up landing on the sand. Then as though this sort of thing happened every day, Jonathan Seagull began his critique of the flight.

"To begin with," he said with a wry smile, "you were all a bit late on the join-up . . ."

It went like lightning through the Flock. Those birds are Outcast! And they have returned! And that . . . that can't happen! Fletcher's predictions of battle melted in the Flock's confusion.

"Well, sure, O.K., they're Outcast," said some of the younger gulls, "but hey, man, where did they learn to fly like that?"

It took almost an hour for the Word of the Elder to pass through the Flock: Ignore them. The gull who speaks to an Outcast is himself Outcast. The gull who looks upon an Outcast breaks the Law of the Flock.

Gray-feathered backs were turned upon Jonathan from that moment onward, but he didn't appear to notice. He held his practice sessions directly over the Council Beach and for the first time began pressing his students to the limit of their ability.

"Martin Gull!" he shouted across the sky. "You say you know low-speed flying. You know nothing till you prove it! FLY!"

So quiet little Martin William Seagull, startled to be caught under his instructor's fire, surprised himself and became a wizard of low speeds. In the lightest breeze he could curve his feathers to lift himself without a single flap of wing from sand to cloud and down again.

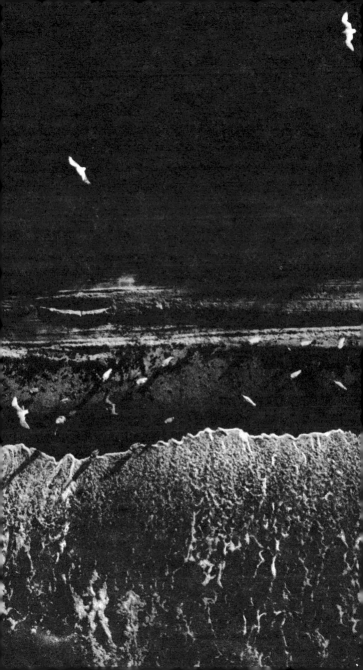

Likewise Charles-Roland Gull flew the Great Mountain Wind to twenty-four thousand feet, came down blue from the cold thin air, amazed and happy, determined to go still higher tomorrow.

Fletcher Seagull, who loved aerobatics like no one else, conquered his sixteen-point vertical slow roll and the next day topped it off with a triple cartwheel, his feathers flashing white sunlight to a beach from which more than one furtive eye watched.

Every hour Jonathan was there at the side of each of his students, demonstrating, suggesting, pressuring, guiding. He flew with them through night and cloud and storm, for the sport of it, while the Flock huddled miserably on the ground.

When the flying was done, the students relaxed in the sand, and in time they listened more closely to Jonathan. He had some crazy ideas that they couldn't understand, but then he had some good ones that they could.

Gradually, in the night, another circle formed around the circle of students—a circle of curious gulls listening in the darkness for hours on end, not wishing to see or be seen of one another, fading away before daybreak.

It was a month after the Return that the first gull of the Flock crossed the line and asked to learn how to fly. In his asking, Terrence Lowell Gull became a condemned bird, labeled Outcast; and the eighth of Jonathan's students.

The next night from the Flock came Kirk Maynard Gull, wobbling across the sand, dragging his left wing, to collapse at Jonathan's feet. "Help me," he said very quietly, speaking in the way that the dying speak. "I want to fly more than anything else in the world . . ."

"Come along then," said Jonathan. "Climb with me away from the ground, and we'll begin."

"You don't understand. My wing. I can't move my wing."

"Maynard Gull, you have the freedom to be yourself, your true self, here and now, and nothing can stand in your way. It is the Law of the Great Gull, the Law that Is."

"Are you saying I can fly?"

"I say you are free."

As simply and as quickly as that, Kirk Maynard Gull spread his wings, effortlessly, and lifted into the dark night air. The Flock was roused from sleep by his cry, as loud as he could scream it, from five hundred feet up: "*I can fly! Listen!* I CAN FLY!"

By sunrise there were nearly a thousand birds standing outside the circle of students, looking curiously at Maynard. They didn't care

whether they were seen or not, and they listened, trying to understand Jonathan Seagull.

He spoke of very simple things—that it is right for a gull to fly, that freedom is the very nature of his being, that whatever stands against that freedom must be set aside, be it ritual or superstition or limitation in any form.

"Set aside," came a voice from the multitude, "even if it be the Law of the Flock?"

"The only true law is that which leads to freedom," Jonathan said. "There is no other."

"How do you expect us to fly as you fly?" came another voice. "You are special and gifted and divine, above other birds."

"Look at Fletcher! Lowell! Charles-Roland! Judy Lee! Are they also special and gifted and divine? No more than you are, no more than I am. The only difference, the very only one, is that they have begun to understand what they really are and have begun to practice it."

His students, save Fletcher, shifted uneasily. They hadn't realized that this was what they were doing.

The crowd grew larger every day, coming to question, to idolize, to scorn.

"They are saying in the Flock that if you are not the Son of the Great Gull Himself," Fletcher told Jonathan one morning after Advanced Speed Practice, "then you are a thousand years ahead of your time."

Jonathan sighed. The price of being misunderstood, he thought. They call you devil or they call you god. "What do you think, Fletch? Are we ahead of our time?"

A long silence. "Well, this kind of flying has always been here to be learned by anybody who wanted to discover it; that's got nothing to do with time. We're ahead of the fashion, maybe. Ahead of the way that most gulls fly."

"That's something," Jonathan said, rolling to glide inverted for a while. "That's not half as bad as being ahead of our time."

It happened just a week later. Fletcher was demonstrating the elements of high-speed flying to a class of new students. He had just pulled out of his dive from seven thousand feet, a long gray streak firing a few inches above the beach, when a young bird on its first flight glided directly into his path, calling for its mother. With a tenth of a second to avoid the youngster, Fletcher Lynd Seagull snapped hard to the left, at something over two hundred miles per hour, into a cliff of solid granite.

It was, for him, as though the rock were a giant hard door into another world. A burst of fear and shock and black as he hit, and then he was adrift in a strange strange sky, forgetting, remembering, forgetting; afraid and sad and sorry, terribly sorry.

The voice came to him as it had in the first day that he had met Jonathan Livingston Seagull.

"The trick, Fletcher, is that we are trying to overcome our limitations in order, patiently. We don't tackle flying through rock until a little later in the program."

"Jonathan!"

"Also known as the Son of the Great Gull," his instructor said dryly.

"What are you doing here? The cliff! Haven't I . . . didn't I . . . die?"

"Oh, Fletch, come on. Think. If you are talking to me now, then obviously you didn't die, did you? What you did manage to do was to change your level of consciousness rather abruptly. It's your choice now. You can stay here and learn on this level—which is quite a bit higher than the one you left, by the way— or you can go back and keep working with the Flock. The Elders were hoping for some kind of disaster, but they're startled that you obliged them so well."

"I want to go back to the Flock, of course. I've barely begun with the new group!"

"Very well, Fletcher. Remember what we were saying about one's body being nothing more than thought itself. . . .?"

Fletcher shook his head and stretched his wings and opened his eyes at the base of the cliff, in the center of the whole Flock assembled. There was a great clamor of squawks and screes from the crowd when first he moved.

"He lives! He that was dead *lives!*"

"Touched him with a wingtip! Brought him to life! The Son of the Great Gull!"

"No! He denies it! He's a devil! DEVIL! Come to break the Flock!"

There were four thousand gulls in the crowd, frightened at what had happened, and the cry DEVIL! went through them like the wind of an ocean storm. Eyes glazed, beaks sharp, they closed in to destroy.

"Would you feel better if we left, Fletcher?" asked Jonathan.

"I certainly wouldn't object too much if we did . . ."

Instantly they stood together a half-mile away, and the flashing beaks of the mob closed on empty air.

"Why is it," Jonathan puzzled, "that the hardest thing in the world is to convince a bird that he is free, and that he can prove it for himself if he'd just spend a little time practicing? Why should that be so hard?"

Fletcher still blinked from the change of scene. "What did you just do? How did we get here?"

"You did say you wanted to be out of the mob, didn't you?"

"Yes! But how did you . . ."

"Like everything else, Fletcher. Practice."

By morning the Flock had forgotten its insanity, but Fletcher had not. "Jonathan, remember what you said a long time ago, about loving the Flock enough to return to it and help it learn?"

"Sure."

"I don't understand how you manage to love a mob of birds that has just tried to kill you."

"Oh, Fletch, you don't love that! You don't love hatred and evil, of course. You have to practice and see the real gull, the good in every one of them, and to help them see it in themselves. That's what I mean by love. It's fun, when you get the knack of it.

"I remember a fierce young bird, for instance, Fletcher Lynd Seagull, his name. Just been made Outcast, ready to fight the Flock to the death, getting a start on building his own bitter hell out on the Far Cliffs. And here he is today building his own heaven instead, and leading the whole Flock in that direction."

Fletcher turned to his instructor, and there was a moment of fright in his eye. "*Me* leading? What do you mean, *me* leading? You're the instructor here. You couldn't leave!"

"Couldn't I? Don't you think that there might be other flocks, other Fletchers, that need an instructor more than this one, that's on its way toward the light?"

"*Me?* Jon, I'm just a plain seagull, and you're . . ."

". . . the only Son of the Great Gull, I suppose?" Jonathan sighed and looked out to sea. "You don't need me any longer. You need to keep finding yourself, a little more each day, that real, unlimited Fletcher Seagull. He's your instructor. You need to understand him and to practice him."

A moment later Jonathan's body wavered in the air, shimmering, and began to go transparent. "Don't let them spread silly rumors about me, or make me a god. O.K., Fletch? I'm a seagull. I like to fly, maybe . . ."

"JONATHAN!"

"Poor Fletch. Don't believe what your eyes are telling you. All they show is limitation. Look with your understanding, find out what you already know, and you'll see the way to fly."

The shimmering stopped. Jonathan Seagull had vanished into empty air.

After a time, Fletcher Gull dragged himself into the sky and faced a brand-new group of students, eager for their first lesson.

"To begin with," he said heavily, "you've got to understand that a seagull is an unlimited idea of freedom, an image of the Great Gull, and your whole body, from wingtip to wingtip, is nothing more than your thought itself."

The young gulls looked at him quizzically. Hey, man, they thought, this doesn't sound like a rule for a loop.

Fletcher sighed and started over. "Hm. Ah . . . very well," he said, and eyed them critically. "Let's begin with Level Flight." And saying that, he understood all at once that his friend had quite honestly been no more divine than Fletcher himself.

No limits, Jonathan? he thought. Well, then, the time's not distant when I'm going to appear out of thin air on *your* beach, and show you a thing or two about flying!

And though he tried to look properly severe for his students, Fletcher Seagull suddenly saw them all as they really were, just for a moment, and he more than liked, he loved what he saw. No limits, Jonathan? he thought, and he smiled. His race to learn had begun.